LIVING IN SPACE

Lucy Bowman and Abigail Wheatley

Designed by Jenny Offley and Tabitha Blore
Illustrated by Rafael Mayani
Additional illustrations by Peter Donnelly

Space consultant: Libby Jackson, Human Spaceflight expert
Reading consultant: Alison Kelly

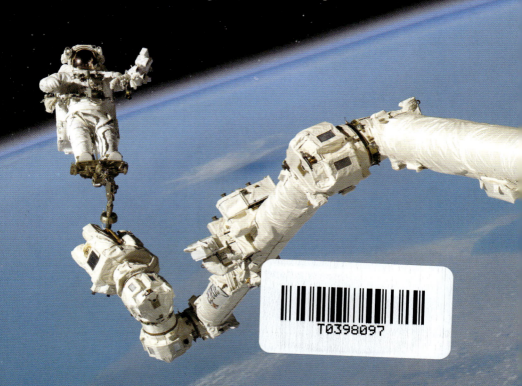

Contents

3 Astronauts
4 Space school
6 Lift off
8 Arrival
10 Inside the ISS
12 Spacesuits
14 Airlock
16 Space walking
18 Hard at work
20 Bedroom and bathroom
22 Keeping healthy
24 Relaxation
26 Back to Earth
28 In the future
30 Glossary
31 Usborne Quicklinks
32 Index

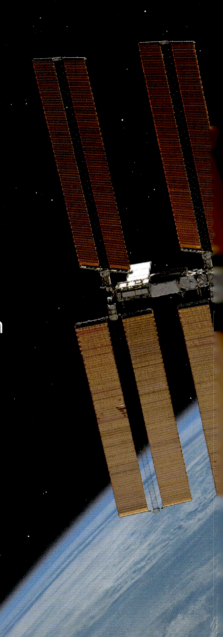

Astronauts

Astronauts are people who travel into space. Most astronauts live and work on the International Space Station (ISS).

This is the ISS. It's a huge spacecraft that travels around the Earth.

Sometimes astronauts go outside the ISS. This is called space walking.

Space school

Before they can go into space, astronauts must train for at least two years.

Astronauts learn how to fly a spacecraft using a simulator.

They get used to working with different types of scientific equipment.

In space everything floats. Astronauts train underwater to get used to the feeling.

Hello   Здра́вствуйте

All astronauts have to learn to speak English and Russian.

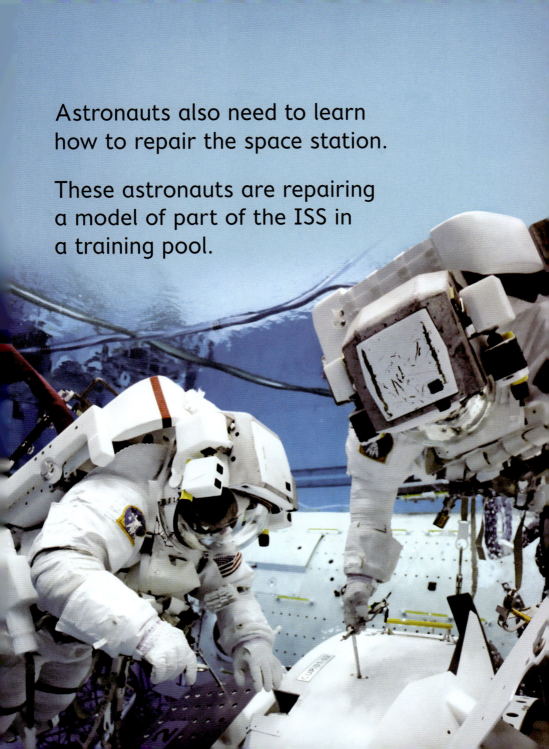

Astronauts also need to learn how to repair the space station.

These astronauts are repairing a model of part of the ISS in a training pool.

Lift off

Astronauts go to the ISS in a spacecraft called Soyuz. It travels into space in a rocket.

Once the rocket reaches space, parts that aren't needed any longer fall away.

1. The booster rockets drop off first.

Nose

The Soyuz spacecraft is in here.

Soyuz

2. The nose cone is next.

3. The rocket's body is last.

There's not much room inside the Soyuz spacecraft.

Booster rockets

Arrival

As Soyuz travels through space, solar panels fold out. They collect energy from the Sun to power the spacecraft.

About six hours after taking off, Soyuz reaches the ISS.

Solar panel

1. Soyuz lines up with a docking port on the ISS.

2. It flies closer very slowly and joins on. Locks hold it in place.

3. A hatch opens on the ISS. The astronauts float on board.

A few times a year, spacecraft carry fresh supplies from Earth to the ISS.

Inside the ISS

The ISS is made up of lots of small rooms joined together. This picture has parts cut away, so you can see inside.

A laboratory for carrying out experiments

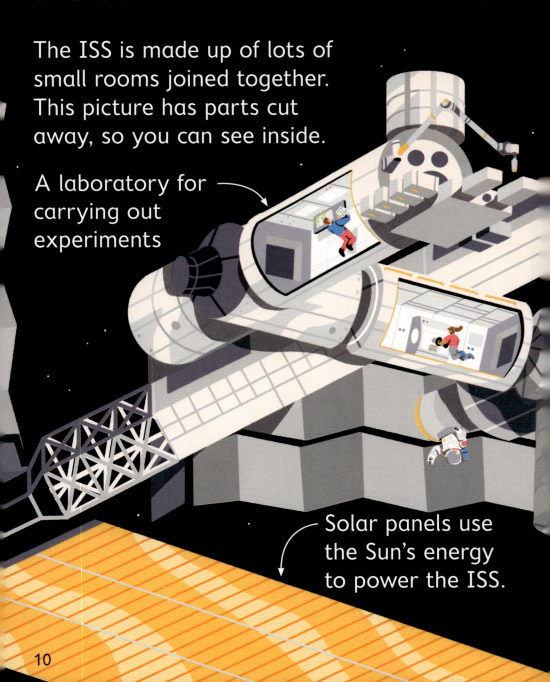

Solar panels use the Sun's energy to power the ISS.

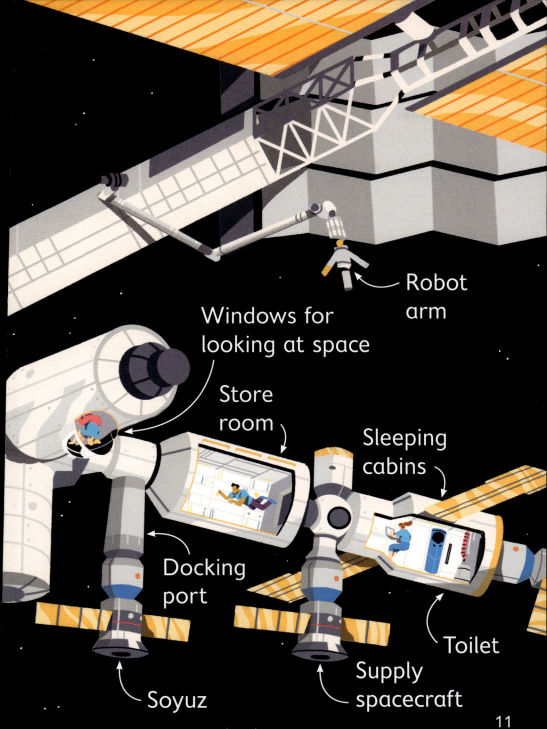

Spacesuits

When astronauts go outside the ISS they have to wear a spacesuit.

1. First they put on a layer that can keep them warm or cool.

2. They then pull on a thick layer over their legs and feet.

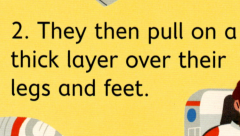

3. A thick top and backpack go on next. The backpack carries air for breathing.

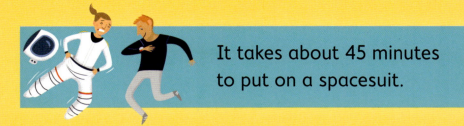

It takes about 45 minutes to put on a spacesuit.

Microphone for talking to other astronauts

4. Gloves and a cap are next. The cap has speakers and a microphone.

5. A helmet goes on last. Tubes bring air from the backpack into the helmet.

Airlock

To get outside, astronauts go through an airlock. It has doors and two small rooms that stop air escaping from the ISS.

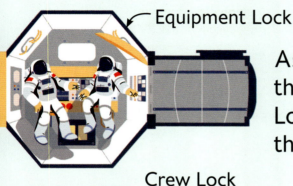

Equipment Lock

Astronauts go into the Equipment Lock and put on their spacesuits.

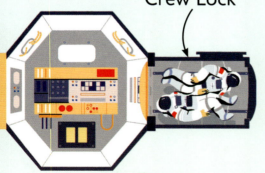

Crew Lock

They enter the Crew Lock next. Air is sucked back into the ISS.

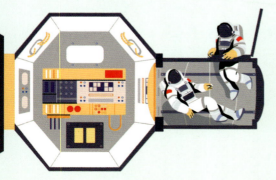

Then they open an outer hatch and go out into space.

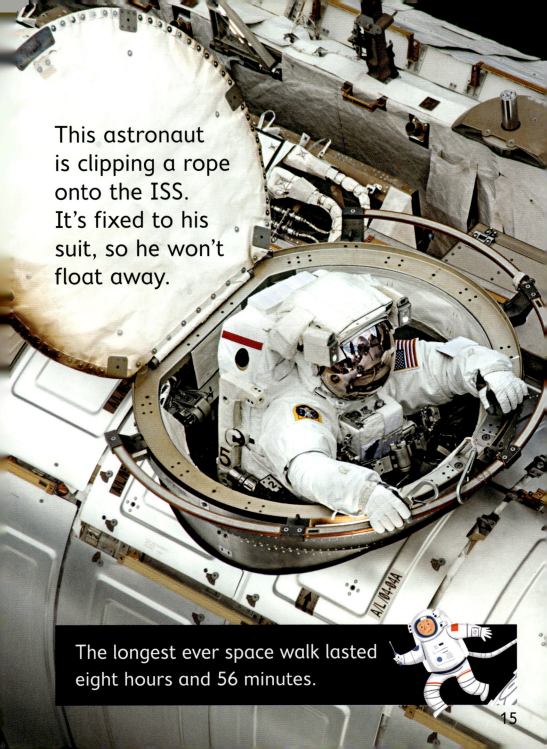

This astronaut is clipping a rope onto the ISS. It's fixed to his suit, so he won't float away.

The longest ever space walk lasted eight hours and 56 minutes.

Space walking

Sometimes, astronauts go outside the ISS to make repairs.

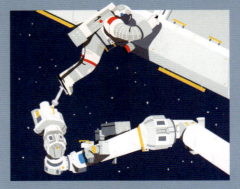

To move short distances, they pull themselves along using hand grips.

They clip their feet to a robot arm. It moves them around outside the ISS.

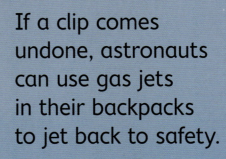

If a clip comes undone, astronauts can use gas jets in their backpacks to jet back to safety.

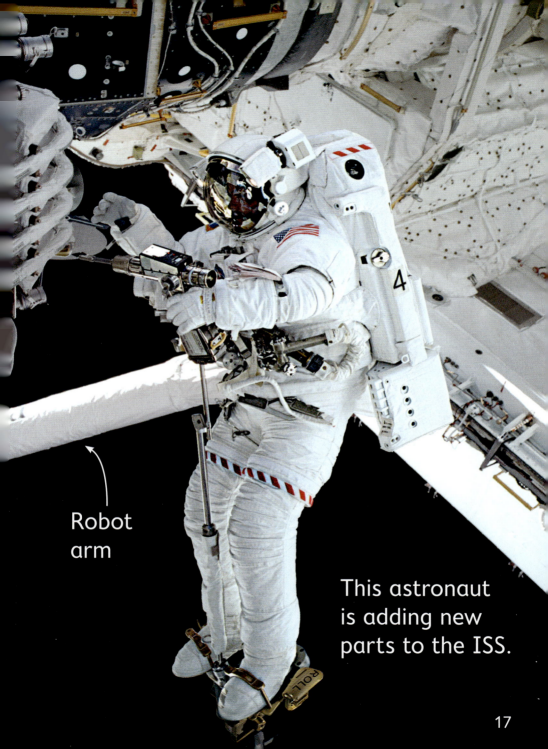

Robot arm

This astronaut is adding new parts to the ISS.

17

Hard at work

Astronauts spend a lot of their time working. They do experiments to find out how different things behave in space.

They study animals such as fish to see what happens to them.

They grow different plants to see which can survive best.

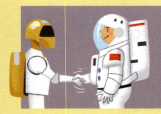

Scientists have built robots that can go into space. One day they might do jobs astronauts do now.

These astronauts are in a laboratory. One of them is testing whether his eyes have changed while living in space.

Bedroom and bathroom

The ISS has tiny cabins to sleep in, and a bathroom.

Astronauts keep their personal things in their sleeping cabin.

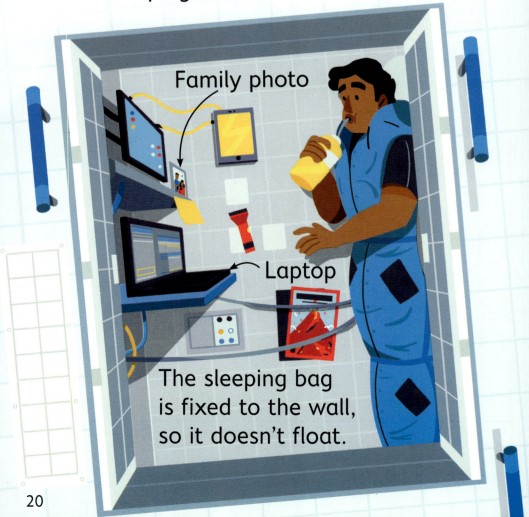

Family photo

Laptop

The sleeping bag is fixed to the wall, so it doesn't float.

In the ISS bathroom, astronauts are careful not to waste water.

They wash with a cloth and just a few drops of water.

Their toothpaste is safe to swallow, so they don't have to rinse it away.

ISS toilets don't flush using water. They suck waste into tanks.

When astronauts trim their nails, they vacuum up the clippings to stop them from floating away.

21

Keeping healthy

Astronauts take care to stay healthy while living in space.

Astronauts exercise for two hours a day to keep their bones and muscles strong.

They eat healthy food. Most of it is kept in pouches so it stays fresh.

They carry out regular checks to make sure they are fit and well.

Sometimes fresh fruit and vegetables are sent to the ISS with other supplies.

This astronaut is keeping fit by running on a machine called a treadmill. He is strapped on so he can't float away.

Relaxation

Astronauts get some time off from work to do things they enjoy.

Some astronauts sing and play musical instruments.

Others watch movies together on a big screen.

They play games with magnetic pieces that can't float away.

Once a week they have a video call with their families.

The Cupola is an area of the ISS with seven windows.

Astronauts spend time there looking at the Earth and taking photos.

Back to Earth

After about six months on the ISS, most astronauts travel back to Earth in the Soyuz spacecraft.

The Soyuz spacecraft sets off from the ISS.

As it gets close to Earth, some parts fall away.

A parachute comes out of Soyuz, slowing it down.

It bounces down onto the ground, then stops.

Doctors and ground crew drive quickly to the spacecraft. They let the astronauts out and make sure they aren't injured or ill.

This snowy landing site is in Kazakhstan, in central Asia.

In the future

One day, people might not just live on the ISS, but on a planet, such as Mars.

Mars is very cold and there's no air. People could live inside a base.

This is how a base on Mars might look.

Fruit and vegetables are growing in here.

These astronauts are wearing spacesuits.

This is the main living area.

All the doors are fitted with airlocks.

Mars is very far away. It would take more than half a year for people to get there.

Glossary

Here are some of the words in this book you might not know. This page tells you what they mean.

 astronaut - someone who travels into space.

 simulator - a machine that trains astronauts to fly space vehicles.

 spacecraft - a space vehicle that astronauts ride or live in.

 hatch - a strong door that astronauts use on a spacecraft and the ISS.

 laboratory - a room with scientific equipment used for experiments.

 Cupola - part of the ISS with windows all around, giving views outside.

 airlock - two small rooms with hatches that stop air from escaping into space.

Usborne Quicklinks

Would you like to find out more about living in space? You can visit Usborne Quicklinks for links to websites with videos, amazing facts and things to make and do.

Go to **usborne.com/Quicklinks** and type in the keywords "**beginners living in space**". Make sure you ask a grown-up before going online.

Notes for grown-ups

Please read the internet safety guidelines at Usborne Quicklinks with your child. Children should be supervised online. The websites are regularly reviewed and the links at Usborne Quicklinks are updated. However, Usborne Publishing is not responsible and does not accept liability for the content or availability of any website other than its own.

This floating robot was sent to the ISS. It took photographs of the astronauts at work.

Index

airlock, 14-15, 29, 30
backpack, 12, 13, 16
bathroom, 20-21
Cupola, 25, 30
docking port, 9, 11
Earth, 3, 9, 25, 26
exercise, 22, 23
experiments, 10, 18-19
food, 22, 28
hatch, 9, 14, 30
laboratory, 10, 19, 30
lift off, 6-7
Mars, 28-29

relaxation, 24-25
repairs, 5, 16
robot arm, 11, 16, 17
rockets, 6, 7
simulator, 4, 30
sleeping, 11, 20
solar panels, 8, 10
Soyuz, 6, 7, 8, 9, 11, 26, 27
space walking, 3, 15, 16-17
spacesuits, 12-13, 14, 15
supply spacecraft, 9, 11
toilets, 11, 21
training, 4-5

Acknowledgements

Senior Designer: Helen Edmonds
Photographic manipulation by John Russell

Photo credits

The publishers are grateful to the following for permission to reproduce material:
Cover © NASA; **1** © NASA/JSC; **2-3** © STS-133 Shuttle Crew, NASA; © NASA; **5** © ESA/NASA; **6-7** © NASA/Bill Ingalls; **8** © Andrey Armyagov/Alamy Stock Photo; **15** © JSC/NASA/Fyodor Yurchikhin; **17** © NASA; **19** © NASA; **21** © NASA; **25** © NASA; **27** © NASA/Bill Ingalls; **28-29** © Bryan Versteeg/spacehabs.com; **31** © JAXA/NASA

Every effort has been made to trace and acknowledge ownership of copyright. If any rights have been omitted, the publishers offer to rectify this in any subsequent editions following notification.

This edition first published in 2021 by Usborne Publishing Limited, 83-85 Saffron Hill, London EC1N 8RT, United Kingdom. usborne.com Copyright © 2021, 2019 Usborne Publishing Limited.
The name Usborne and the Balloon logo are registered trade marks of Usborne Publishing Limited.
All rights reserved. No part of this publication may be reproduced, stored in a retrieval system or transmitted in any form or by any means without the prior permission of the publisher.
First published in America 2021. This edition published 2024. UE.